SOCCER

Written by

Kay Robertson

rourkeeducationalmedia.com

Scan for Related Titles and Teacher Resources

© 2014 Rourke Educational Media

All rights reserved. No part of this book may be reproduced or utilized in any form or by any means, electronic or mechanical including photocopying, recording, or by any information storage and retrieval system without permission in writing from the publisher.

www.rourkeeducationalmedia.com

PHOTO CREDITS: Cover Alexander Raths © ; Title Page © CEFutcher; Page 4 © Stepan Kachur; Page 5 © Travois; Page 6 © Eric Simard; Page 7 © Gaby Kooijman; Page 8 © Shirell Delaney; Page 9 © Amy S. Meyer; Page 10 © Showface; Page 11 © Amy S. Myers; Page 12 © CEFutcher; Page 13 © Peter Muzslay; Page 15 © CEFutcher; Page 16 © James Boardman; Page 17 © Muzsy; Page 18 © James Boardman; Page 19 © Louis Horch; Page 21 © Joyfull\

Editor: Jill Sherman

Cover Designer: Tara Raymo

Interior Designer: Jen Thomas

Library of Congress PCN Data

Soccer/Kay Robertson
Fun Sports for Fitness
  ISBN 978-1-62169-854-8 (hardcover)
  ISBN 978-1-62169-749-7 (softcover)
  ISBN 978-1-62169-956-9 (e-Book)
Library of Congress Control Number: 2013936459

Rourke Educational Media
Printed in the United States of America,
North Mankato, Minnesota

rourkeeducationalmedia.com

customerservice@rourkeeducationalmedia.com • PO Box 643328 Vero Beach, Florida 32964

Table of Contents

Basics of the Game 4

Soccer Gear 7

Kicking the Ball 9

Dribbling the Ball 12

Passing the Ball 14

Trapping the Ball 17

Protecting the Goal 20

Special Kicks 22

Glossary 23

Index 24

Websites 24

Show What You Know 24

Basics of the Game

Soccer is one of the most popular participation sports for athletes of all ages the world over. The international name for soccer is football, though it in no way resembles American football. The sport got its start in England and Scotland in the 1800s. Today more boys and girls in the United States play soccer than any other single sport.

The popularity of the sport is shown by the massive crowd packing this stadium.

A standard soccer field, or pitch, is 110 to 120 yards (100.5 to 109.7 meters) long and 70 to 80 yards (64 to 73.1 meters) wide. Permanent lines mark the space in front of each goal, which are called the goal areas. Larger rectangles outside these goal areas are called the penalty areas.

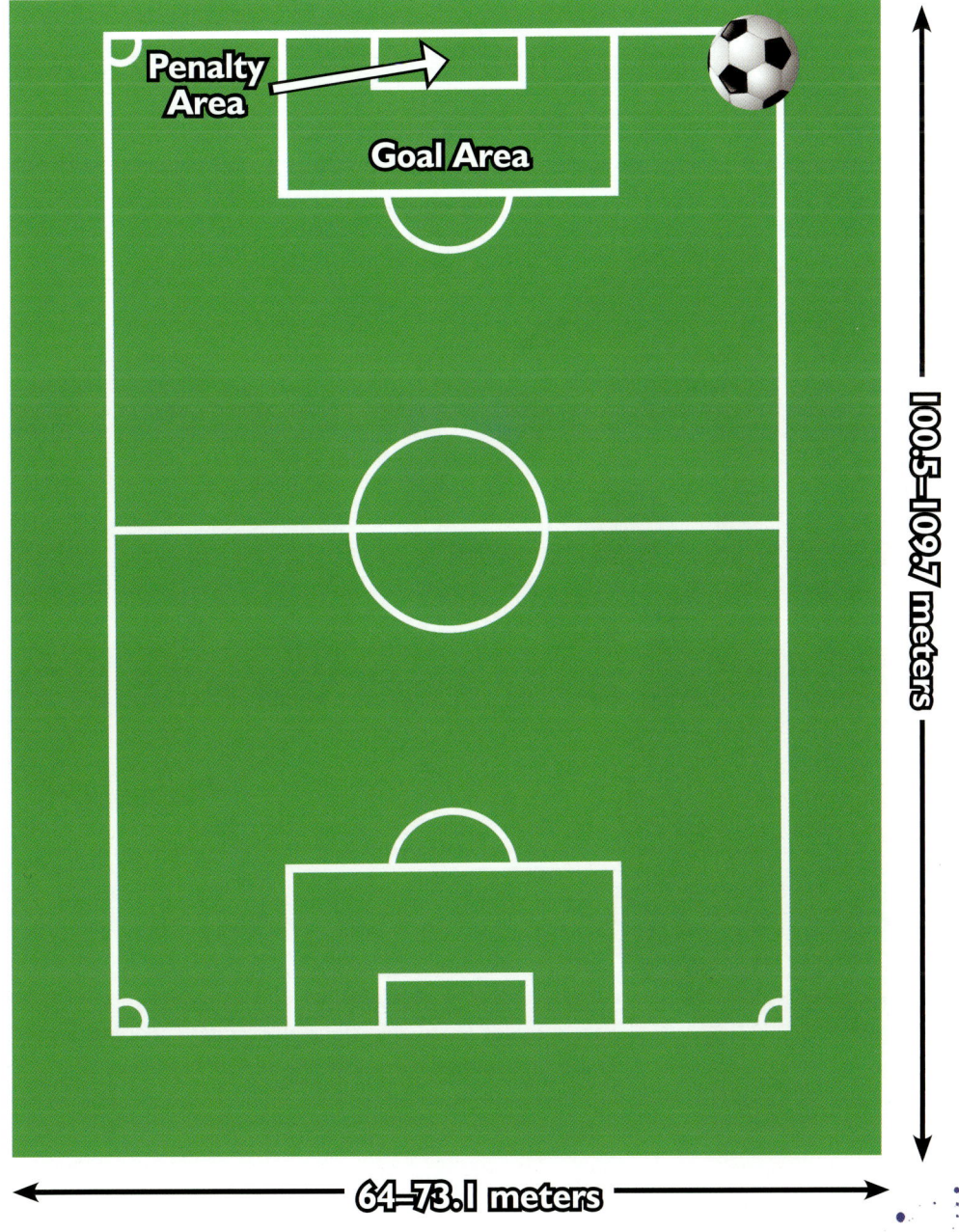

Each team typically fields 11 players. In a standard 4-3-3 formation, there are four defensive backfielders, three midfielders, and three strikers, plus the goalkeeper. The game is played in two 45-minute halves of running time, although the clock does not stop when play is halted. The referee may add time at the end of each half to make up for delays if players are injured.

> Some historians say the word "soccer" came from English schoolboy slang. It came about as an abbreviation of the word "association" from Association Football.

Soccer builds leadership skills, encourages teamwork, and brings real enjoyment to players of the sport.

Soccer Gear

Soccer can be played informally with almost no special equipment. The modern soccer ball is constructed of **synthetic** materials, is very light, and lasts a long time. At more organized levels, players wear cleated, or spiked, shoes for better footing and plastic guards to protect the shins.

Soccer balls from the late 19th century were made of leather panels and were so heavy that "heading" the ball could cause serious injury.

With the extra grip that cleats provide, the player is able to turn and keep their footing at high rates of speed.

Kicking the Ball

The key to moving the ball in soccer is proper footwork, or kicking. Players use the front and both sides of each foot to direct the ball and to apply spin when shooting or passing.

Good balance is **fundamental** to successful footwork. This is partly achieved by keeping the head still when kicking. Strong legs are another must for any serious soccer player. Running, biking, stair climbing, and jogging all contribute to building strong legs.

The striking point for kicking the ball is the top, or instep, of the foot, not the toes. Imagine kicking with the laces of your shoes. Whether shooting or passing to a teammate, try to place the non-kicking foot beside the ball to avoid hitting too far in front of or behind the ball.

Kicking the ball takes more than just your foot. Strength comes from the entire leg, as well as from proper body rotation.

Unlike tackling in American football, which requires actual physical contact, tackling in soccer means taking the ball from an opponent without physical contact.

One of the most exciting and difficult kicks in soccer is the bicycle kick. This is typically **executed** by a striker very near the opponents' goal. With his or her back to the goal, the shooter must throw his or her legs high into the air and kick the ball while falling backward, and then land safely.

The kicker places her left foot beside the ball and will strike the ball with the top of her right foot.

Dribbling the Ball

Dribbling is the fine art of controlling the ball at any speed while a defender tries to take it away from you. Dribbling is used in soccer, just as it is in basketball, to move the ball around the field of play. Soccer players may not use their hands, however, only their feet.

Learning to dribble with confidence can be a difficult and time consuming exercise. It can also make the difference between a good player and an excellent one. Speed and agility will come with practice. Just remember to keep the ball as close to your feet as possible.

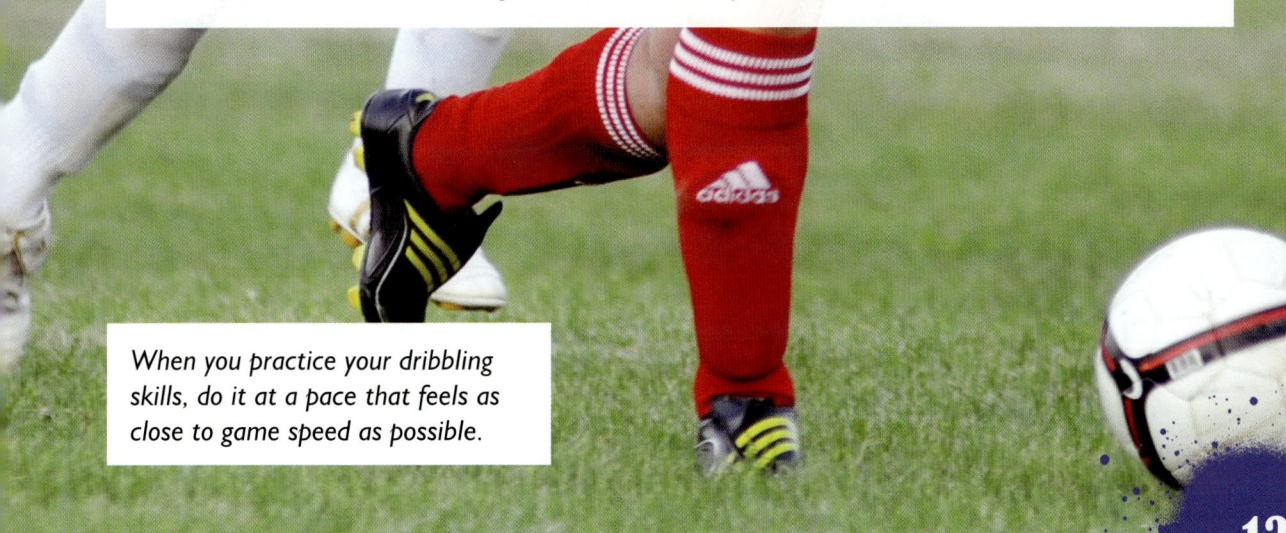

When you practice your dribbling skills, do it at a pace that feels as close to game speed as possible.

Passing the Ball

Next to **honing** skills as a shooter, no weapon serves the soccer player better than the art of passing the ball. This requires not only physical ability, but also a keen awareness of the field. Above all else, soccer is a team sport. A team-first attitude among all players is a must.

Since soccer is a running game, practice passing the ball to moving objects rather than **stationary** ones. A good passer not only puts the ball in the area where a teammate is currently stationed, but also leads that teammate to a spot where he or she is about to arrive.

Many experts agree that one of the most important things about any team sport isn't winning, but the friends you make and teamwork skills you learn.

Speed is important, but so is concentrating on the spot where you want to pass the ball.

You cannot use your hands to make a pass. However, it is perfectly acceptable, once you master the skill, to use your head to redirect the ball.

Trapping the Ball

There are two ends to every pass, the sender and the receiver. Since you can't use your hands to catch the ball, trapping it is the next best thing. This is done by clamping one foot down on the top of the ball as it arrives, damping its energy before it bounces away.

Trapping is a good way to control the ball, especially when your opponent is trying to take control of it.

If you're positioned in such a way that the ball arrives at an angle, use either the inside or outside of your foot to trap the ball against the ground. In all cases, this **maneuver** should be done quickly and smoothly. This will allow the flow of play to continue and help you avoid tacklers.

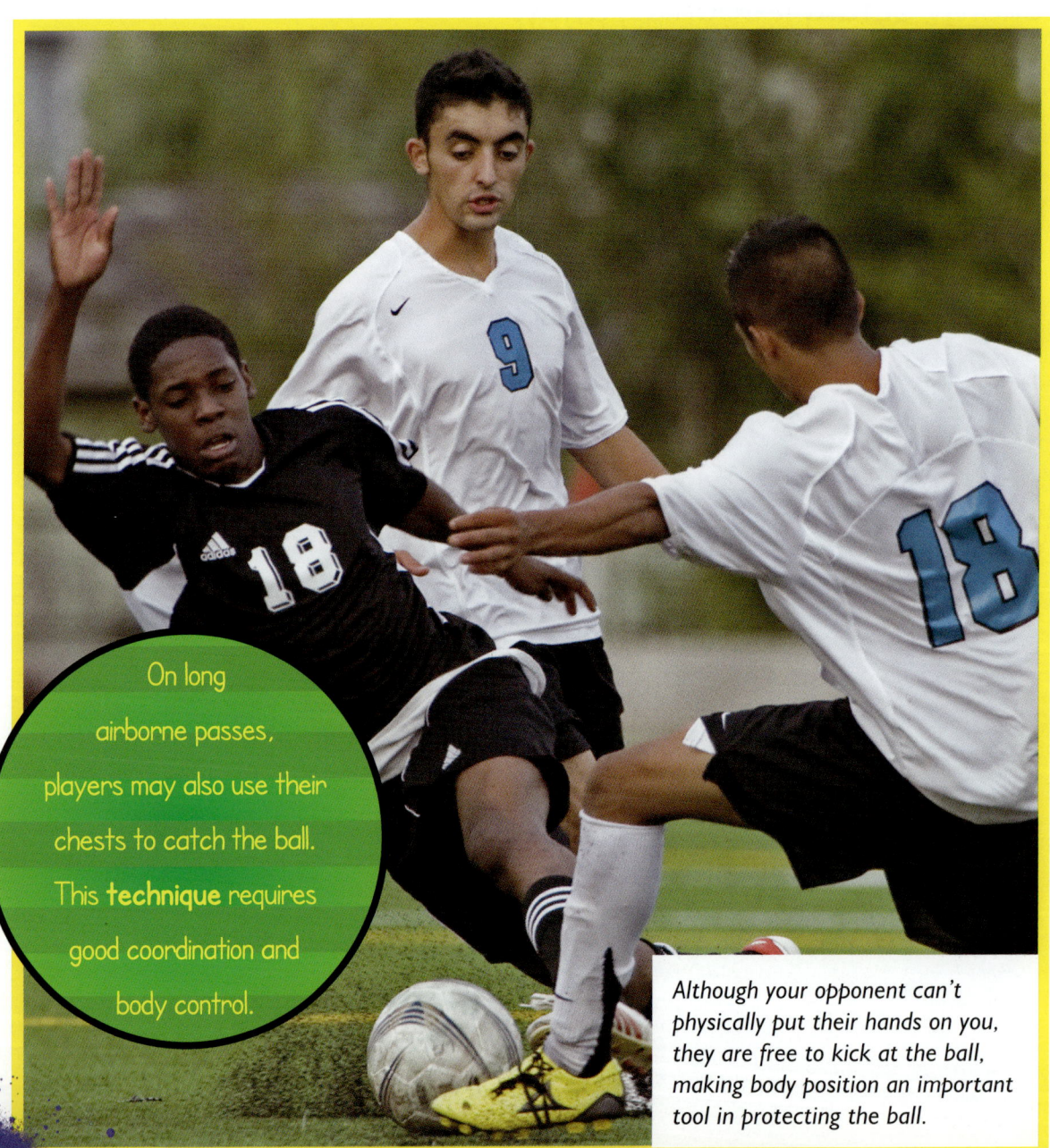

On long airborne passes, players may also use their chests to catch the ball. This **technique** requires good coordination and body control.

Although your opponent can't physically put their hands on you, they are free to kick at the ball, making body position an important tool in protecting the ball.

18

Being in the right place at the right time will make you an even more effective soccer player.

Protecting the Goal

No player is more in the spotlight than the goalkeeper. As the last line of defense, the goalie's mistakes can turn the tide of a game. Standing before the gaping 8 x 24 foot (2.4 x 7.3 meter) goal cage, even the most gifted keeper can feel small and **vulnerable**.

Unlike the other 10 players on the team, the goalkeeper is allowed to catch and hold the ball to stop play. However, the keeper must get rid of the ball in a timely manner. This can be done by passing the ball overhead, rolling it on the ground, or punting it downfield to a distant teammate.

Goalkeepers wear a different color jersey from those worn by their teammates. This is so the referee can easily determine in a scramble who is handling the ball. The goalie may also wear specially designed gloves to avoid broken fingers and to increase grip on the ball.

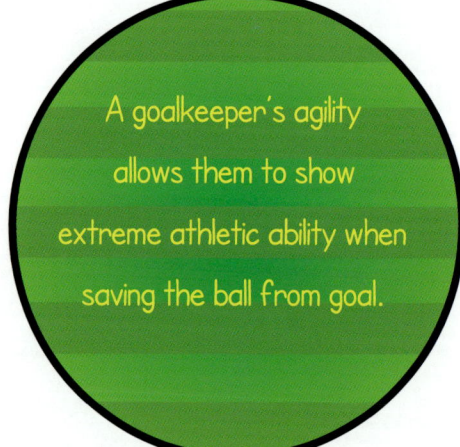

A goalkeeper's agility allows them to show extreme athletic ability when saving the ball from goal.

Special Kicks

Penalty kicks are awarded if a defender in the 18 foot (5.5 meter) box in front of his own goal commits a foul, such as pushing or tripping. The offended team chooses a player to attempt the kick, which is then made from the spot of the foul with only the goalkeeper to beat.

Similar to a penalty kick, a free kick is awarded after a foul. The free kick may either be direct or indirect. A direct kick is a shot on goal. In an indirect kick, however, two players must touch the ball before a shot on goal is taken. In either case, the defending team retreats 10 yards (9.1 meters) from the point of the kick.

A corner kick is awarded when the defending team puts the ball out of bounds behind its own goal. The ball is placed in the triangle in the appropriate corner of the field. A player adept at slicing or arcing the ball has a pretty good chance at scoring on a corner kick. The corner kick is an exciting moment in any soccer match, with a goal, or even the final score on the line.

Glossary

executed (EX-eh-KYOO-ted): carried out, put into effect, performed

fundamental (fun-da-MEN-tal): a basic, essential element

honing (HONE-ing): perfecting or making more intense; sharpening

maneuver (mah-NOO-ver): a physical movement requiring skill or dexterity

stationary (STAY-shun-airy): not moving; fixed in place

synthetic (sin-THET-ick): not of natural origin; manmade

technique (TECK-NEEK): the skill shown in a performance

vulnerable (VUL-ner-ah-bul): in a position to absorb possible injury

Index

Association Football   6
backfielders   6
bicycle kick   11
dribbling   12, 13
football   4, 10
goalkeeper(s)   6, 20, 22
kicking   9, 10, 11
midfielders   6
passing   9, 10, 14, 20
penalty areas   5
penalty kicks   22
referee   6, 20
soccer ball   7
soccer field   5
striker(s)   6, 11
trapping   17

Websites to Visit

www.soccerwebsite.org/kids_soccer_websites.html

www.kidsfirstsoccer.com

www.kidssoccerworld.com

Show What You Know

1. What is it called when you move the ball with your head?
2. Why does the goalkeeper wear a different jersey than the other players on the team?
3. How many halves are there in a soccer game?
4. What is a penalty kick?
5. What does it mean to trap the ball?